NO THRONE FOR TWO

A Journey Through Love, Betrayal, and Redemption

Sarah M. Aletile

Dedication

This book is dedicated to every woman who's ever loved too deeply and forgot herself. To the ones who stayed when they should have walked away. It is for the hearts that carried silence when they deserved to be heard, and for the souls who are learning that their worth is not up for negotiation.

May you find yourself again in these pages, and may you rise stronger, softer, and whole.

Acknowledgement

Firstly, I return all the glory to God the Author of my story; the one who held me when love failed and gave me the courage to heal.

To my spiritual Mentors and Covering, thank you for teaching me to stand even when Life felt Heavy. Your prayers and wisdom shaped me not only on this journey but as a woman.

To my Editor Mr. BAH JEFF NDUM, Co-editor Ms. VICTORY NINTAI, and my PUBLISHER, thank you for believing in this work, refining my raw words into pages that flow with clarity and grace giving it wings to reach beyond me.

To my family, your unwavering support and unending prayers is woven into every page of this Book. And also Thank you My ZCGC Cyprus Family.

Finally, to every reader who opens these pages, thank you. Your presence here is proof that no story is wasted and no broken heart is beyond REDEMPTION. May you find peace and healing of your own in these words.

PART ONE

THE BEGINNING

Page Intentionally left bank

CHAPTER ONE

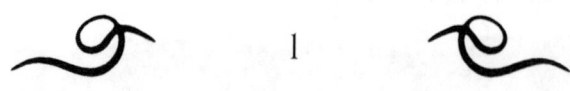

THE BEGINNING OF US

**Sometimes the beginning feels like a promise,
but it's only a preview.**

Before him, I was fine, whole even.
But there was a softness in me that longed for more than
strength.
I wanted presence, a voice that didn't fade;
A love that didn't make me feel like,
I had to shrink to fit into someone's life.

Then he came, not loud, not dramatic.
Just…there.
With a presence that spoke louder than his words.
He wasn't the type to sweep me off my feet
but something about him made me stand still.

He laughed with his chest,
looked me in the eye when I spoke,
and held space for my thoughts like they mattered.

And I remember thinking:

"Maybe this time, love won't hurt."

We started like an unspoken poem.

No labels, no pressure, just energy; Connection.

That warm pull when two souls find each other in the

dark.

I used to catch him watching me,

like I was something worth studying.

He'd say things like:

"You're peace. You calm me."

And I'd melt;

I'd always wanted to be someone's safe space

not just their escape.

And sometimes,

when you've been starved of love,

even the idea of "possible"

is enough to make you stay.

No Throne For Two

There were late-night conversations
about dreams we hadn't spoken out loud before.
He told me about his past,
like he was handing me broken glass.
And I held every piece like it wouldn't cut me.

I showed him my scars.
Not just the ones life gave me,
but the ones love had left behind.
And he didn't flinch.

There was one night, wrapped in sheets and soft music,
where he whispered:
"You're not like the rest. You're resourceful, real; kind.
You're the kind of woman I don't ever want to lose."
And I believed him.

Sometimes,
we don't fall in love with the person,
we fall in love with their potential to protect us from what
hurt before.

But even then…Even in the beginning…
There were moments he hesitated.

Moments where I gave a little more than he reached for,
And I ignored it.
Because when you crave connection,
even crumbs can feel like a feast.

*"Sometimes the beginning feels like a promise,
But it's only a preview."*

I didn't know what was coming.
I didn't know how much my heart would stretch, or break.
After many betrayals, failed promises; trials and errors,
He was like a divine gift from God;
It was like a, "Joy at Last" moment.

But in that moment;
in that soft; quiet, beginning
I was just a woman hoping this time,
love would be different.

His voice cut through the emotional chaos in me
Like a calm I didn't know I was waiting for.
And when he smiled, something in me whispered,
"Maybe this time, love won't break me."
We weren't perfect, but we were possible.
And sometimes, that is enough.

CHAPTER TWO

OUR GLORY DAYS

Real love isn't always loud. Sometimes, it whispers between shared glances and quiet spaces.

There was a time when we laughed more than we
questioned.
When the world outside could crumble,
and it still felt like we had everything we needed;
In the looks, in the touches,
in the way our fingers found each other
like they were always meant to intertwine.

He knew how to disarm me;
His smile was a language only I understood.
He'd pull me close without asking,
and I'd melt into him
like it was the safest place on earth.

We didn't need much,
a playlist, some takeout, the couch.

We could sit in silence and still feel like something
important was happening.
He'd joke about how I was "too serious,"
and I'd call him "too playful."
And somehow, it worked.

He softened my edges.
I sharpened his Dreams.

"Real love isn't always loud.
Sometimes,
it whispers between shared glances and quiet spaces."

I remember the way he'd call me baby
like it was his favourite word.
The way he'd tell me he liked how I thought,
not just how I looked.
He listened to my dreams like he wanted to be part of
them.

No Throne For Two

One night, he looked me in the eye and said:

"You're different. You're not just someone to pass time with.

You're the kind of woman that makes a man change everything."

He made me believe I was the one.

Not just another chapter but the story.

We had our songs, our inside jokes;

our little things that made no sense to the world

but meant everything to us.

He showered me with gifts and surprises,

And in that moment, I thought:

"Maybe this is what love is;

presence, not promises."

He would say:

"You're not just someone I want,

you're an angel sent to me.

You're someone I need in order to become better."

And in those moments, I believed him.

No Throne For Two

I wrote his name in my journal,

Prayed over him without him knowing.

Believed in him in ways he hadn't learned to believe in

himself yet.

When I love;

I love with my hands, my heart, and my hopes.

I do not love halfway,

I do not love on accident.

There were sunsets I'll never forget.

Smiles that felt eternal.

Moments when we were just us,

free from expectations and past pain.

And maybe that's what made the later pain so sharp.

We had something real

or at least it felt that way.

And real is rare.

CHAPTER THREE

THE CRACKS

**When silence becomes the safest way to keep
peace, Love has already started bleeding.**

It didn't fall apart all at once,

that's the hardest part to explain.

It was in the pauses;

The way his responses took longer;

the way I started checking his energy before speaking.

I realized I had stopped asking questions

not because I trusted too much,

but because I feared the answers.

*"When silence becomes the safest way to keep peace,
Love has already started bleeding."*

He used to text me good morning

like I was the first thought in his day.

Then one morning,

I woke up to silence and it didn't stop there.

Suddenly, his phone was always upside down.

Suddenly, he had "so much on his mind."

Suddenly,

I was "overthinking."

I'd ask where he was and he'd get defensive.

He'd say;

"You don't trust me anymore."

But how…

How could I trust what had become a moving target?

We were speaking on the phone one night when he said:

"I'll call you back shortly,

I have to handle something real quick."

Hours passed,

No call; No message.

I sat there,

phone in hand, eyes wide open; chest tight

realizing I was loving someone who made me feel

forgotten in real time.

No Throne For Two

That night changed me.

"Heartbreak isn't just what they do to you.
It's how often they make you question your own worth
While you are still holding onto them."

I told myself,
"Maybe he's tired.
Maybe it's stress.
Maybe I'm just being too sensitive."
Women like me stretch and cover.
We love like it's our duty
to carry what they don't even admit they're dropping.

In all these, God started to whisper louder than my
excuses.
He started pulling me back to myself,
started showing me that sometimes,
the red flags aren't on the battlefield
they're in the patterns.

No Throne For Two

I noticed a shift in his tone.
A sharpness where gentleness used to live.
He laughed less and I cried more.
Slowly, I became the only one trying.

Still praying,
Still hoping,
Still staying.

"When love feels like chasing,
It's no longer mutual
It's survival."

Women like me don't walk away from something we
prayed for.
Not even when it starts to feel like punishment.
Deep down I knew something was breaking,
not just between us, but in me.
And I didn't want to lose myself just to keep someone
who didn't know how to hold me anymore.

Page Intentionally left bank

PART TWO

THE BREAKING

CHAPTER FOUR

THE LIES WE LIVED

**When you have to beg for clarity, you already
know the truth.**

There's a silence that screams louder than shouting.
It comes when the person you love looks you in the face
and lies, and you know it.
You feel it in your chest,
you hear it in their tone,
your spirit shifts and suddenly
even their love feels foreign.

*"When you have to beg for clarity,
You already know the truth."*

I knew something was off before he said a word,
the way he avoided my eyes.
The sudden change in his schedule,
the *"I forgot to call"* becoming the new normal.

No Throne For Two

There was a night I saw some traces light up on his phone
And for the very first time,
I requested to see his phone.
He swore it was nothing serious,
And I need not worry about it.
I asked again and this time,
his answers came out crooked and shaky.
He was hiding something.
My heart knew
I didn't need proof; I felt it.
I knew he wasn't fully mine anymore.

But I still stayed hoping;
Hoping love could cover what truth had already revealed.

"Love makes you patient.
But lies make you paranoid."

We had a fight, but not the usual kind.
It wasn't about socks on the floor or unanswered calls.
It was about me asking if I was still his.

No Throne For Two

I said:

"I feel like you're slipping."

"Like I'm holding onto someone who's already let go."

And he said:

"Why can't you just trust me?"

"Why do you always assume the worst?"

Love shouldn't feel like assuming anything.

It should show up,

it should confirm itself. Daily.

He said I was everything to him,

that he didn't want to lose me.

That if he could rewind time,

he'd choose me over and over again.

But if that was true,

why did his actions feel like rejection on repeat?

Don't tell me I'm your dream woman if you keep treating

me like a backup plan.

Still, I held on.

I held on because we had history.

No Throne For Two

Because I saw pieces of good in him when we first met,
I thought healing him would help heal me.

But the truth is
You can't fix someone who benefits from your brokenness.
You can't grow love in soil watered by dishonesty.

The night I finally let myself break was the night I
realized:
He may never be honest enough to tell me the full truth.
But God already had.
And that was enough.

CHAPTER FIVE

AFTER THE STORM

You can love someone deeply and still choose yourself. That's not betrayal, that's Survival.

The first few days after it all cracked,

I didn't cry as much as I expected.

However, I felt hollow.

Like I had been emptied out

and left behind by someone who once called me home.

There were no calls, no explanations,

Just space,

Cold;

An unfamiliar space.

But in that space, I started to hear God more clearly.

I stopped waiting and hoping.

Instead, I opened my Book of Holy Covenant and God's

promises (**THE WORD**).

I lit a candle and whispered into silence:

No Throne For Two

"FATHER, was that love or a test?"

Sometimes God removes who you thought you needed

To remind you of who you are without them.

I began to pour my heart into my journal instead of his

text messages.

Pages soaked in ink and prayer.

"Heal me, God.

Not just from him but from the version of me who accepted less."

I sat with my pain like it was a teacher,

Didn't numb it, didn't deny it

Just breathed through it,

one deep breath at a time.

I started noticing how much energy I used to pour into his

potential but now,

I was pouring it back into my Peace.

There was no firework in this chapter.

Just quiet healing, long walks,

And Worship music at 2AM.

No Throne For Two

I slowly realized that I had made him my center,
When GOD was always supposed to be on the THRONE.
I confused his attention for affection
His charm for commitment, his apologies for change.
I no longer needed to hear why he did what he did.
God already revealing what I needed.
That some people love you for what you give
not who you are.
And I am not here to be used
I am here to be honored.

I asked less about what he was doing,
and more about what God was doing in me.
It wasn't an easy phase of Life.

Slowly,
I started becoming someone I hadn't met in a long time.
A woman who loved herself more than her desire to be
chosen.

No Throne For Two

You can love someone deeply and still choose yourself.
That's not betrayal, that's Survival.

So, I packed my hope,

my tears and my prayers,

and I left.

Even though it broke my heart

I knew it was time.

CHAPTER SIX

THE RETURN

**When someone knows how to break you, they
usually know how to sound like healing too.**

It always happens like this
just when you're starting to breathe differently,
just when your chest is no longer tight with grief.
They come back.

Not always with flowers.
Sometimes just words, a simple text;
"Hey. Can we talk?"
And your heart flinches.
Because it remembers everything,
but part of you still wants to hear them out.
Just once, just to see if maybe it wasn't all lies.

He said,
"I can't stop thinking about you."
"I miss you. I don't want to lose you."

No Throne For Two

And part of me softened,

Because after the pain

he still knew how to speak to the part of me that never

stopped hoping.

When someone knows how to break you,

They usually know how to sound like healing too.

He said I was his dream woman.

That if he ever saw me with someone else,

it would destroy him.

That I was the one he'd choose again and again if he

could turn back the clock.

He promised patience,

said he was ready to show up,

asked me to trust him just one more time.

And I wanted to,

God knows I did.

But my spirit had questions my heart was afraid to ask.

So, I asked him:

"What am I to you now?"

"Are you asking for me or just missing the feeling of me?"

Because clarity is love,

if you say I'm yours then say it with your actions this time,

not just your regrets.

"Don't return if your heart is still divided.

I am not a vessel for your in-between.

There is no throne for two."

He said he didn't want to play games.

That he didn't want to see me with anyone else.

That I was helpful, peaceful,

the one who brought out the best in him.

But my soul whispered,

"Can a man love you deeply and still dishonor you?"

And the answer hung heavy in the air:

Yes.

Because sometimes love isn't enough not if it's not honest,

Not if it still confuses you.

I told him.

"If you want me, then want me all the way.
Choose me loudly, clearly and consistently.
Because I'm not standing in the grey anymore
I've cried too many nights there."
"I forgave you, but I also forgave myself
For staying too long the first time."

He said,

"I'll prove it."

So, I watched.

Not just what he said, but what he did.

Because this time,

my heart needed evidence not just emotion.

PART THREE

THE AWAKENING

CHAPTER SEVEN

THE FRAGILE REBOUND

Love can be resurrected, but only if truth is the foundation.

Getting back together doesn't mean picking up where we
left off.
It means choosing to meet again,
in a different version of ourselves,
hopefully wiser, hopefully softer, and hopefully honest.

But it was hard not to wonder:
Was this Love reborn or just recycled?
He came back with effort.
Not grand gestures, just presence.
He called more, checked in, asked how I was really doing,
and I saw a piece of the man I first fell for again.

He said,
"I know I hurt you.
But I want to make this right."

No Throne For Two

"If you're patient with me, I'll show you I've changed.
I have learned,
grown to love and trust you with my Life and all I have."

I wanted to believe that maybe love could grow again
not on top of what broke us, but through it.

Love can be resurrected,
But only if truth is the foundation.

Still,
there were moments that tested my spirit.
Because even though we were sharing laughs and late-
night calls again,
my heart was tired with assumptions.
I needed definition,
commitment with clarity.

He said:
"You're mine.
You always were. I just got lost

No Throne For Two

But I want to do right by you this time."

And I wanted to hold onto that.

But the woman I had become wasn't just listening with

her ears

She was listening with discernment.

Some days felt beautiful again.

We laughed like we used to,

he'd kiss my forehead saying things like:

"You stuck beside me, even when I didn't deserve it"

But my spirit still held its breath,

trauma doesn't just leave when love returns.

It lingers, asks questions, looks out for patterns, studies in

silence.

You can forgive someone

And still not feel fully safe with them again,

Healing is not the same as forgetting.

I prayed often.

"God, if this is real, confirm it with peace.

And if it's just another cycle
Give me the strength to walk away for good."
Because this time,
I wasn't begging to be chosen
I was watching to see if he was willing to choose me.
Consistently, clearly, and completely.

One night, he held my face in his hand and said,
"You're not just a good woman.
You're the woman I want to become a better man for."
And I smiled, but deep down,
I whispered to myself,
"We'll see."

CHAPTER EIGHT

RELAPSE OR REDEMPTION

You should never have to shrink your needs to fit someone else's comfort.

The thing about second chances is they feel like hope at
first.

Like fresh air after holding your breath too long

But the deeper truth is…

Hope can feel a lot like denial when you ignore your gut.

At first, everything felt better

He was around more,

Gentler, intentional even.

He'd say, *"I'm proud of you."*

"I see you doing your thing."

"You make life easier, lighter."

And I believed him. Or at least, I wanted to.

But something started shifting again

The scarce replies came back,

No Throne For Two

The *"I've been busy"* lines,

the mood swings that had no real explanation.

One minute I was his peace

the next he was distant like we were Strangers again

and in that moment, he wanted to keep it like that.

"I don't want to lose you again.

I want to make it right by you," he said.

Consistency is not too much a thing to ask for.

You should never have to shrink your needs to fit someone else's
comfort

You see, redemption takes work.

Not just words or, showing up once or twice

but changing patterns.

And love without real change is just a rerun of pain.

If he keeps making you question yourself

While convincing you it's love,

it's not healing, but MANIPULATION.

So, I prayed deeply.

"Dear heavenly father,
if this is where it ends don't let me stay out of fear.
Don't let me confuse familiarity with purpose."

And God answered.
Not with thunder but with Peace.
A peace that felt like release.

I finally realized,
yes, he came back;
Yes, he said the right things.
But words without true transformation
will always lead you back to the same kind of end.
And this time I loved myself enough to choose clarity over
Chaos.

No Throne For Two

CHAPTER NINE

THE EXIT, THE FREEDOM

You can love someone with all your heart, and still know when it's time to let go.

There's a difference between

leaving because you're defeated,

And leaving because you've finally learned to appreciate

your Value.

Knowing what exactly you want

And also, how far you can go if you just be yourself is

important.

I left him.

I left because I choose myself more.

The last time we spoke,

his voice was softer than usual.

The apologies came again,

the promises of *"I'll do better."*

"I don't want to lose you."

No Throne For Two

But I already knew the truth:

You can't lose something you never truly owned.

And love doesn't feel like a threat every time it's tested.

I asked him one last time:

"What are you offering me now?"

And for the first time in a long time,

I didn't need an answer.

I already had my own.

I was offering myself PEACE.

I was offering myself CLARITY.

And I was offering myself FREEDOM.

I am not afraid of walking away anymore.

Because staying in confusion is far more dangerous than

Leaving with a broken experience.

No more excuses,

No more promises.

I said:

"I loved you when I felt loving myself wasn't enough

But I've learned better now.

I won't settle for less than what I deserve.

And that's peace, honesty,

and love that grows not fades."

Then he said calmly:

"I hope one day you'll forgive me."

And I nodded.

Because I had forgiven him long before I walked away

Despite every ill word

And untrue narratives he put out there.

The hardest Part wasn't leaving

It was realizing I had to forgive myself for staying too

long.

I didn't feel angry or bitter

I just felt so FREE.

Free to be me.

To rebuild and trust again.

And this time,

It would be a trust I built with God and myself first.

Know that there's power in choosing yourself,

even when you loved someone deeply.

You can love someone with all your heart,
and still know when it's time to let go.

And so, I walked away.
Not as the woman who was broken
But as the woman who had finally remembered who she
was.
And that woman is…
She was enough.

Reflection:

A Prayer for Healing and Growth

I stand here today, not as the woman I was before,

But as the woman I've always been.

Strong, resilient, loved, and free.

I no longer seek for validation from the past,

because my worth was never tied to someone else's

approval.

Heavenly Father,

Thank you for every tear I shed

For every night I stayed awake,

Wondering if I would ever heal from the pain

Thank you for the strength you gave me when I thought I

had none,

And for showing me that PEACE doesn't come from a

person,

But from knowing You, Father.

I've learned that love is not about filling the void,

but about growing whole

And allowing another to walk alongside me.

Not complete me

But to walk with me on the path you've set.

"ABBA, I pray that the next chapter of my Life be filled

with grace,

peace and divine connections.

May I continue to choose myself every day

and may I always remember that

Healing is not linear, but it is Beautiful.

As I turn the page to the next chapter,

I carry neither shame nor guilt,

Only lessons learned and strength earned."

Closing Message:

A Letter to My Readers

To those of you who've walked with me through these papers. Thank you for opening your heart to my story. I hope it reminded you of something important. That no matter how many times you fall, you have the power to rise.

You have the right to love yourself fiercely, even if it means walking away from the ones who couldn't see your worth. Love is beautiful, but it must be rooted in honesty, respect and consistency. You deserve a love that calls you Higher, not one that keeps you chained to your doubts.

So, to anyone who is still finding their way, I say this, *"Choose yourself, and Trust that God has a love for you that is greater than any lie. Let go of what doesn't serve you, and make space for the person you were meant to be."*

Your heart is worthy of a love that sees you fully, not in pieces. And once you realize that; You will never "settle" again.

THE END.

FEATURED
PIECES

THE LIGHT I FOUND

This is not a story of loss. It is a story of becoming whole
again.

We played together like teenagers in love,
I opened my soul, unfolded every secret, hid nothing.
We were perfect, or so I thought.
You were the air I breathed,
my knight in shining armour.

I believed my soul had found its mate.
We dreamt of forever,
You said life was nothing without me,
called me your peace and yet, chose war.
Love costs nothing, yet with you it drained me.

I left from being your favourite person to call,
to someone you forgot about for days.
Is this the love you promised?

No Throne For Two

I lost myself;

I became a shadow fading in silence.

No light, no hope,

only tears in an ocean of pain you left me in.

Were your words lies?

The feeling I thought was love

Was actually chains on my soul.

Depression whispered "the end,"

And death knocked at my door.

If I had clung to you,

Would I ever have found the peace I hold today?

So, I ran.

I ran to my Creator,

I ran as fast as my weary heart could go.

And there…

There I found the light.

God met me in my brokenness,

wrapped me in a peace unshaken

and became my everything:

My beginning, my ending, my reason to live again.

You were never my forever, God was.

Now I rise,

bold and unafraid,

a daughter of victory,

a soul reborn in love unbreakable.

ANITA. I. EJIOGU

No Throne For Two

A HARLOT'S LOVE STORY

(Glass crashing)

I had never felt my heart sink so deep.

Fear froze me,

unsure whether to flee

or move to pick up the broken pieces.

"He must've just been too upset," I told myself.

"A bad day at work. Maybe the traffic was too much."

But this was my lover. This was my lover.

I reminded myself.

We made it through that night.

He smiled a little too much,

As if trying to erase the beast I had just seen.

"Babe, are you okay?"

Suddenly, I thought harder before answering.

Suddenly, I breathed quieter.

No Throne For Two

But still, I told myself:
He is my lover. He is my lover.

The day he hit me broke something in me.
It was a small disagreement;
I had raised my voice just a little, trying to be heard.
But before I could finish my sentence,
the room turned pitch black.
Sounds bounced from ear to ear;
my brain rang like a warning bell.
That night, I cried until I couldn't anymore.
I grabbed a pillow and screamed my heart into it.
My soul shattered into a million pieces,
and I couldn't find most of them.
That was the end of it. **Chapter closed.**

When the next chapter opened,
I thought I was wiser.
I raised my shoulders higher, smiled less;
threw tantrums when I deemed fit.
But this time, my new lover didn't respond.

No Throne For Two

He just nodded, quietly,
always agreeing.

I thought I felt safe with him.
I thought this was different. But it wasn't.
No punches were thrown,
but this lover was anything but faithful.
He had cousins, sisters, family friends,
and somehow
they all left lipstick stains on his shirt.

So, I loved him harder.
Gave my body like a sacrifice whenever he sought
pleasure.
But no matter how much I gave,
I just wasn't enough.

So, I got louder, angrier,
hoping this love would hear me.
But it never did.
It apologized; countless times,

but it was anything but sorry.

So, I moved. **Chapter closed.**

Just when I had given up on love,

another chapter opened.

This one was tough but handful.

Never showed me commitment.

I guess I shouldn't expect that from married men.

But with this love, I learned to be content.

I told myself maybe the fairytale just wasn't written for

girls like me.

I had seen every shade of selfish love,

and I was ready to settle for the least toxic of them all.

Then one day I met this woman. Gomer.

The harlot who carried anything in her loins but shame.

The wife whose children bore names after her promiscuity,

whose husband wrote love poems on tear-soaked pages,

hoping, praying, waiting.

A woman whose body was an open battlefield

No Throne For Two

And yet, wore no armor of regret.

The day I met her;
I squeezed my face in disgust,
And spat on the ground beside her,
because all I could see was filth.
I scoffed.

But as I turned to leave, something happened.
Her husband walked in.
Straight to the counter with no hesitation,
Paid the price for her bounty like it was nothing.
Then, with the joy of a man receiving the world,
he walked forward, arms open, smiling wide
to pick up his bride.

My jaws dropped.
I was still in shock when I realized,
that woman was me.
For years, I had been loved selfishly.

No Throne For Two

I had been told what love was supposed to look like,
but it was never this reckless, never this real.
That a man could be so captivated
by the presence of a woman who had broken his trust too
many times to count...
It didn't make sense.

I sat in the front row of church
and listened as the preacher told this Gomer tale.
And suddenly,
my heart began to yearn for more.
I wanted a love like that,
a love that holds my heart with both hands.
A safe space;
with no lies and no secrets to hide.

I longed peace,
peace that surpasses all understanding,
that sets a weary heart at rest.

That was the love I found in Jesus.

And even though I'm still waiting;

Waiting for a love that will hold me like this one I've

found,

best believe this time,

I won't be settling for less.

NINTAI VICTORY

MY LOVER

On the floor of the restroom,

Pinned into a corner, I cuddle myself.

The world was silent and I alone existed.

Yet, not I.

I clawed at my toenails;

And with my hands

One palm over the other,

Pressed against my mouth

So no one heard the songs my heart sang.

And no, not from pleasure.

That I can assure you.

Those songs were catalysts

Sparking a reaction

That flowed down my cheeks

With every aching heartbeat.

No Throne For Two

I said to myself:

Leave this floor.

The floor of the restroom

Was not where I belonged.

Yet the floor of the restroom

Was my pinnacle.

At the pinnacle of brokenness

That is where my true Lover,

My Groom,

Waits for His bride.

But you see,

All along I chased a different groom

A groom whose love I had to ask for.

I chased his love

Like a dehydrated traveler

Stranded in the desert.

His love was the water I thought I needed to quench my
thirst
Forgetting I had the River that never runs dry.
And so I begged for just a drop.

I tasted a drop.
The good morning text messages,
They were lovely.
They made my heart flutter,
My legs wiggle;

Like a babe seeing his mother's face at dawn,
Or like the joy a little girl feels in the arms of her first love,
Her dad.
"Can we have dinner tonight
And later, chill at my house?"
Dinner, maybe
But what does "chill" even mean?
Those words sent chills down my spine.

How can you claim love
When you don't even know what it looks like?

Love isn't explained in the sheets of his bed.
It's written on the sheet of paper
That says John 3:16
Not him on me.

And it wasn't enough.
Because the love I desire, no man can quench.
It's the type of love paid for with blood.
For the Father to willingly give His Son
For the Son to choose to lay His life

One offered a way
The other became the way.
My true lover does not impose, He guides,
Directs and instructs.
He leaves the choice to me, cause
Is it truly love If I don't choose Him every day?
I had neglected His love in search of butterflies for my

belly,

I had neglected His love in search of highs

Cause the Lows were uncomfortable but you see,

That low, is where my Lover waits.

ATA LYDIA

HEARTBREAK AND GOD

When the heart stops, a man dies;

Luckily, mine only broke.

But my hands were too frail to pick up its fragments.

Death smiled as the doctor said to dad,

"You have cancer;

It's spread to your brain, and you have few days to live."

I sank into grief,

I felt like a needle thrown into an ocean;

no one could find me.

It felt like nails being drilled into my once-whole heart.

Dad went to heaven a few days later.

I feared the pieces of my heart wouldn't be found,

my eyes poured down oceans,

and my voice lost its life.

This was grief.

In my pain I heard the Lord say,

No Throne For Two

"Death doesn't kill, my child,

it only moves a person to his next location."

I wondered what those words meant.

It seemed like fire had met ice,

I melted.

Those words felt like a magnet,

bringing my pieces together;

in my grief,

peace stepped in;

the Lord stepped in.

I remembered dad reading the scriptures to my siblings

and I.

He loved to read the scripture that says,

"Blessed are those who mourn for they will be comforted,"

is this what he meant all along?

Was I experiencing the comfort of the Lord?

It suddenly occurred to me that grief was a door.

One that gave me access

to embrace the comfort of the Lord.

I wish I wouldn't have to mourn

but I began to ask the Lord,

"What is life to a believer?

My love has gone

and so, I'm scared.

I don't want to have kids and they get to feel this pain I'm

feeling."

Death seemed to have broken my heart.

In pain, I heard the Lord say:

"Life is a journey.

It's like a man sent on an errand,

the place he is sent to is not home

and so, he can't be too comfortable there.

He must not forget the will of the master who sent him.

I am your Father

and I have sent you to the earth

to mirror my nature and will to a broken world.

I want to bring a dying world back to life

and so, death is not the end for you my child,

it's just the exit door by which you return back to me
from the errand I've sent you on."

I had never heard words so pure and powerful,
this was comfort,
one that restored me back to my essence;
one that pulled me out of the grave I lived in;
one that lifted the weight of hurt I bore for years;
one that dressed me as Christ's bride.

The Lord opened up His heart to me,
He showed me a part of Him I heard of and never
experienced,
Now, I rejoice in Papa's death.
For though I grieve,
I am filled with joy.

For he ran the race and endured to the end,
he fought the good fight of faith
and I know He will hear the words
"Well done, my good and faithful servant."

TREASURE CAULCRICK